In the Den

and

Mick and Mum

By **Elizabeth Dale**   Illustrated by
Giusi Capizzi

The Letter N

Trace the lower and upper case letter with a finger. Sound out the letter.

Down,
up,
around,
down

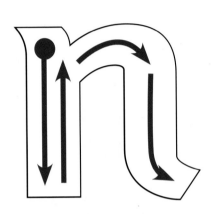

Up,
down,
up

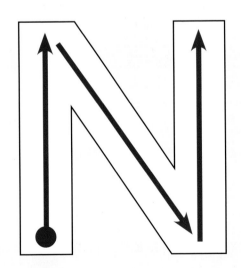

Some words to familiarise:

den   Meg   Mick

High-frequency words:

in   a   me   is   the

it   no   he   his   on   of

Tips for Reading 'In the Den'

- Practise the words listed above before reading the story.
- If the reader struggles with any of the other words, ask them to look for sounds they know in the word. Encourage them to sound out the words and help them read the words if necessary.
- After reading the story, ask the reader who the den belongs to.

Fun Activity

Build a den for a toy out of cardboard!

In the Den

Rob sits in a den.

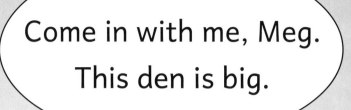

Meg sits in the den.

Rob, Meg and Tom sit
in the den.

It is big! It is such fun.

But Mick comes in. He is big.
He wags his tail.

15

Mick sits in his den...

The Letter M

Trace the lower and upper case letter with a finger. Sound out the letter.

*Down,
up,
around,
down,
up,
around,
down*

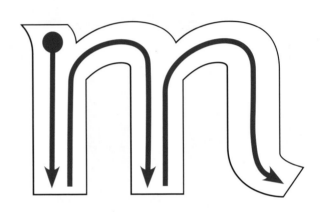

*Up,
down,
up,
down*

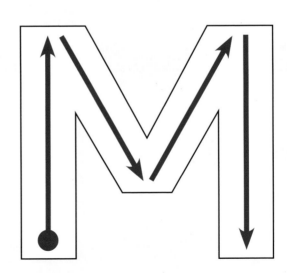

Some words to familiarise:

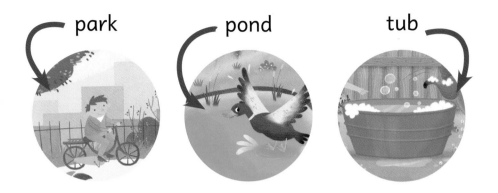

park   pond   tub

High-frequency words:

go   to   the   no

Tips for Reading 'Mick and Mum'

- Practise the words listed above before reading the story.

- If the reader struggles with any of the other words, ask them to look for sounds they know in the word. Encourage them to sound out the words and help them read the words if necessary.

- After reading the story, ask the reader why Mum wanted to get Mick wet at the end of the story.

Fun Activity

Draw another way Mick could get wet.

Mick and Mum

Mick and Mum go to the park.

Mick and Mum go to the wood.

Mick and Mum go to the zoo.

Mick and Mum go to the pond.

29

Book Bands for Guided Reading

The Institute of Education book banding system is a scale of colours that reflects the various levels of reading difficulty. The bands are assigned by taking into account the content, the language style, the layout and phonics. Word, phrase and sentence level work is also taken into consideration.

Maverick Early Readers are a bright, attractive range of books covering the pink to white bands. All of these books have been book banded for guided reading to the industry standard and edited by a leading educational consultant.

To view the whole Maverick Readers scheme, visit our website at www.maverickearlyreaders.com

Or scan the QR code above to view our scheme instantly!

Pink
Red
Yellow
Blue
Green
Orange
Turquoise
Purple
Gold
White